To my husband, John. My best friend and supporter.

- Denise Kaminsky

www.mascotbooks.com

CPSIA Code: PRT0713A
ISBN-10: 1620863472
ISBN-13: 9781620863473

Printed in the United States

NITTANY LION™
Tells the Legend of
Princess Nit-A-Nee

Quiet Please

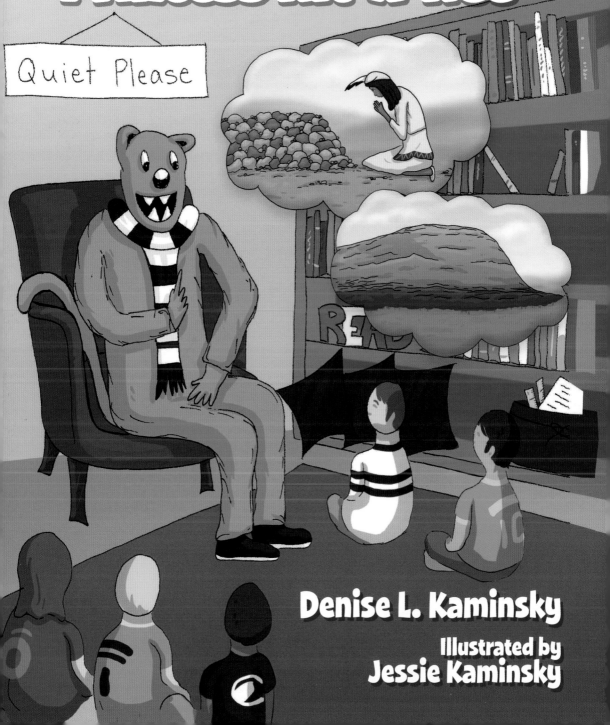

Denise L. Kaminsky

Illustrated by
Jessie Kaminsky

"Hello, Nittany Lion. Thank you for coming to the library. The children love it when you come for Story Time," said Mrs. Chester, the librarian.

"I'm always glad to come," answered Nittany Lion.

"Right this way," said the librarian. "The children are waiting for you."

"Great," he said.

They walked to the Children's Room.

The boys and girls were sitting quietly on the rug. As soon as they spotted Nittany Lion they waved and quietly called, "Hi! Hello! Yeah!"

Nittany Lion waved back, flicked his ears, and shared high-fives with a few of the children.

Nittany Lion found the special Reader's Chair and made himself comfortable. He asked the children, "Do you know what Nittany means?"

The boys and girls looked at each other.
No one knew.

Jake yelled out, "No!"

Nittany Lion put his finger to his lips to remind everyone to use their soft, inside voices.

Nittany Lion asked, "Who was Princess Nit-A-Nee?"

Again, the young boys and girls shook their heads and shrugged their shoulders.

"Well," said Nittany Lion, "I'm here today to tell you the Legend of Princess Nit-A-Nee. Ready?"

Heads bobbed up and down and the children settled themselves for the story.

Nittany Lion began, "Long ago, Native Americans lived in Central Pennsylvania. They were members of the Algonquian-speaking tribes. Nit-A-Nee is Algonquian for 'single mountain.' Nit-A-Nee could also mean 'barrier against the wind,' like how a mountain blocks the wind."

"Over the years, the legend or folklore says Nit-A-Nee was also the name of a Native American princess. Nit-A-Nee loved a young man, a brave named Lion's Paw. She was very sad when he was killed in a battle.

After the battle, Nit-A-Nee picked up Lion's Paw."

"She carried the courageous brave to his grave in the center of their wide, broad valley. Nit-A-Nee covered his body with stones and soil. This was a mound of honor for his strength and to show her love for him."

"On the last night of the full moon, Princess Nit-A-Nee finished adding soil and stones to the high mound over Lion's Paw. Then, a terrible rainstorm began. There were great bolts of lightning and loud blasts of thunder. Strong winds roared through the valley. All the members of the tribe shuddered and looked at Lion's Paw's mound. They saw Princess Nit-A-Nee standing on the burial mound with her arms outstretched. It was like she was reaching for the lightning bolts in the sky."

"Next, according to the legend, everyone watched in awe all through the night. Lion's Paw's burial mound magically grew higher and higher. At dawn, they saw that it had risen into a high mountain right in the center of the valley. Princess Nit-A-Nee was gone. Standing on top of the mountain was a big lion with eleven orphaned, young male cubs. They were all as brave as Lion's Paw. Each had the heart and strength of Princess Nit-A-Nee."

"It is said that from then on, every place in the valley was safe because the fearless lions roamed as heroes from the mountain. The people of the valley were very happy."

Several of the children clapped.

Nittany Lion continued, "Years later, when others came to this valley, they found happiness. They decided to build a college at the foot of this mountain. The college students showed much strength and courage whenever the winds of destiny and fate blew down on them." Nittany Lion added, "May this strength and courage stay strong in all of us here."

"I'm strong," called Brandon.

"I'm brave," said Emma.

"Glad to hear it," said Nittany Lion.
"I'm strong and brave, too. I am proud
to be named Nittany Lion to remind everyone
of the legend of Princess Nit-A-Nee."

"Yay!" called the children as they jumped up
to hug Nittany Lion.

Many years after Princess Nit-A-Nee disappeared, in 1904 to be exact, Penn State baseball player Harrison D. "Joe" Mason became upset when rival Princeton flaunted a statue of its Bengal tiger during a game. Mason worked to establish the ferocious mountain lion as their good-luck mascot. Calling him the Nittany Lion seemed natural. And, another legend was born.

Mount Nittany

Elevation: 2,077 ft. (633 m)
Location: Centre County, PA, USA
Range: Appalachian Mountains
Topo Map: USGS State College Quadrangle
Climbing: White Trail (easiest)

Reference: Mount Nittany conservancy (http://www.mtnittany.org/)

THE END

ABOUT THE AUTHOR

Denise graduated from Penn State ('73 EKED) and then received a Master of Science in Reading. She was a reading specialist and a third grade teacher. She authored *Nittany Lion Has the Hiccups* and *Nittany Lion Gets a Big Surprise*. Denise is the mother of two grown children, Jay and Jessie (PSU '06 EKED). Jessie is the illustrator of *Nittany Lion Gets a Big Surprise*. Currently, Denise lives in Pennsylvania with her husband, John. They are big Penn State fans.

Have a book idea?

Contact us at:

Mascot Books

560 Herndon Parkway

Suite 120

Herndon, VA

info@mascotbooks.com | www.mascotbooks.com